PHILIP PULLMAN

NORTHERN LIGHTS
THE GRAPHIC NOVEL
VOLUME TWO

Adapted by Stéphane Melchior
Art by Clément Oubrerie
Colour by Clément Oubrerie and Philippe Bruno
Translated by Annie Eaton

DOUBLEDAY

DOUBLEDAY

UK | USA | Canada | Ireland | Australia
India | New Zealand | South Africa

Doubleday is part of the Penguin Random House group of companies
whose addresses can be found at global.penguinrandomhouse.com.

www.penguin.co.uk
www.puffin.co.uk
www.ladybird.co.uk

Penguin
Random House
UK

First published in 2015 by Gallimard Jeunesse as *Les Royaumes du Nord: 2*
This edition published 2016

Adapted from *Northern Lights*, first published by Scholastic UK Ltd, 1995

001

Text of the original work copyright © Philip Pullman, 1995
Adapted text and art copyright © Gallimard Jeunesse, 2015
Translation copyright © Annie Eaton and Philip Pullman, 2016

The moral right of the author has been asserted

Set in 11/12pt Draftsman Casual
Printed in China

A CIP catalogue record for this book is available from the British Library

ISBN: 978–0–857–53463–7

All correspondence to:
Doubleday
Penguin Random House Children's
80 Strand, London WC2R 0RL

Rescued by the gyptians,
Lyra is travelling north to find Lord Asriel
and to save her friend Roger . . .

Lyra thought she was an orphan, but recently learned that
Mrs Coulter and Lord Asriel are her true parents.

The alethiometer, a rare instrument
that allows the reader to find out the
truth, was entrusted to Lyra by the
Master of Jordan College.

Lord Asriel, who is investigating the
mysterious substance known as Dust, is
being held prisoner by armoured bears in
remote Svalbard.

Mrs Coulter, Head of the General
Oblation Board, is probably also behind
the child-snatching Gobblers.

Roger, Lyra's best friend, has been
kidnapped by the Gobblers.

John Faa, King of the gyptians, is leading an expedition north
to rescue the children taken by the Gobblers.

Farder Coram, the oldest of the gyptians, revealed to Lyra the
identity of her true parents. He once saved the life of a witch —
whose help will prove invaluable.

For my father, Claude.
— S. M.

Friendly wishes to P'murr, and to J.J. and Gégé, who, each in their own way,
have given me a love of wide snowy spaces.
— C. O.

The word *dæmon*, which appears throughout this book, is pronounced demon.

Do the Lapland witches live here at Trollesund, Farder Coram?

they live in forests and on the tundra. Their business is with the wild, but they keep a consul here.

Lord Faa told me you were friends with a witch.

Let's say there's an obligation there.

That's why we're here now, to claim the favour.

How did you meet her?

It was over forty years ago . . .

I was alone on my boat, fish

A terrible cry made me look up.

I saw a woman falling out of the air . . .

. . . pursued by a g red bird like nothir seen before.

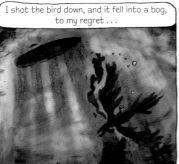

I shot the bird down, and it fell into a bog, to my regret . . .

The woman was like to drowning, but I got her on board.

She was beautiful. But the most extraordinary thing was that she ha no dæmon.

IMPOSSIBL Everyone has dæmon.

That's what I thought too. It gave me a hideous turn.

Later I discovered that witches have the power to separa their selves from their dæmons. And it's my belief that t great red bird I shot was another witch's dæmon, in purs

2

If all that happened over forty years ago, the witch must be as old as you now?

Don't be fooled . . .

. . . witches live three or four times longer than we do.

Thank you for receiving us so promptly, Dr Lanselius.

You are very welcome. But I didn't imagine I had a choice, Farder Coram.

You are correct, sir. But it is still a pleasure to see you.

Careful, the Witch-Consul doesn't like questions.

I should tell you that Serafina Pekkala is now queen of a witch-clan in the region of Lake Enara.

Only answers.

I would like to see her again.

I know that. And I know other things besides.

or example . . .

A group of children arrived here a week ago under the care of the so-called Northern Progress Exploration Company and moved out again the day before yesterday.

Don't ask me where they went.

I'm not asking.

3

Your cup is empty, my dear.

Thank you, sir. And I've been wondering . . . If I had a chance to ask a question of the Witch-Consul, I wonder what the wisest question would be?

An indirect question! You crafty thing!

Well, I might ask where I could obtain the services of an armoured bear.

IMPOSSIBLE!

Aren't the armoured bears in the service of the Oblation Board?

What?

Insolence!

To as
ques

The interview is ended!

I'm sorry . . . I couldn't help myself . . .

STOP!

Talk to us! We en't here for fun — this is a question of life and death!

Well done, Lyra. You must know how to break the rules when an obstacle is put in your way. You are just as I hoped you would be.

Follow me.

 …e witches use sprays of cloud-pine for flying.

 One of these has been used by Serafina Pekkala, and the others have not. Could you tell which is hers?

 You can ask me questions, I see.

But of course.

 Pff . . . They all look the same.

Shush, I'm concentrating.

 You mustn't tell her . . .

. . . but the witches have talked about this child for centuries past.

 …have spoken of a child who has a destiny that can only be fulfilled here – not s world, ar beyond.

…ut this child, we shall all die.

 This is the one, I'm sure!

Remarkable! Who taught you to read the symbols?

 I taught myself. Did Serafina Pekkala really fly with this?

Yes, when she was a child.

 Take this sprig of pine, keep it near, and the witch will know how to find you, wherever you are.

 The bear you need is called Iorek Byrnison, and you'll find him at the sledge depot. He's a renegade. Take care – unlike me, he is a creature of an uncertain temper. Ha ha!

I'm wondering if the Witch-Consul was giving me some kind of test?

The bear? He works over there . . . he's either there or he's drinking at Einarsson's Bar.

Thank you, most kind.

I wouldn't be surprised. I think he was testing both of us, child.

Go to hell.

He was horrible! And I couldn't see his dæmon — I wonder why?

It must have been really tiny, probably a louse.

Is that you, Iorek By the renegade be

Iorek Byrnison, can I speak to you?

What's he doing? Why isn't he answering you?

I don't know.

ROAAA

DAMNED CHILDREN! ALWAYS HARASSING ME!

PEACE!

We only wis speak with

6

Who
you?

I'm Farder Coram, from the gyptian people of Eastern Anglia. And this is Lyra Belacqua. We want to offer you employment.

I am employed.

They say you're a drunkard.

So what?

You're not worthy of being a panserbjørn.

What kind of work are you talking about?

We're moving north, in search of children who have been taken captive. We need your protect—

HEY!

And what will you pay?

gold, if that's what you want.
t interested,
go away!

Forgive me for asking, Iorek Byrnison . . .

Lyra, do we really need him? He's a brute!

. . . but you could live a free proud life on the ice, hunting seals and walruses, or you could go to war and win great prizes. What ties you to Trollesund?

The men here took my armour away, and have turned me into their slave.

Oh . . . I'm beginning to understand.

Tell me where my armour is and I will serve you, either until I am dead or you have a victory. That is my promise. The price is my armour.

I'VE GOT IT!

I know where his armour is!

Oh! But look at this, Lyr

An armoured bear without armour . . . a drunkard to boot . . . No news from Serafina . . . The Witch-Consul was mocking you.

You think so, John? What about this aëronaut of yours what is he, a gambler, a gunfighter from Texas, stuck here in Lapland?

Lee Scoresby knows how to fight . . . and he owns a hot-air balloon!

A hot-air balloon could be really useful!

Just stop being so pessim

QUICK, COME AND LOOK!

The Aurora!

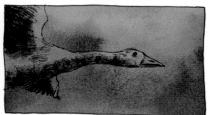

I'm happy and proud to see you again, Kaisa.

Serafina Pekkala sends her greetings to you. She is well and strong.

The great John Faa and the famous Lyra Belacqua, I believe? You are talked about among the witches.

We are searching for the children who were taken. Will the witches help us?

The place you seek is called Bolvangar. It is three or four days north-east of here.

I'm afraid that many of witch-clans are working the Dust-hunters—

Tell me, Ka

— but not Serafina and her clan.

. . . why do the witches talk about me?

Because of your father, and his knowledge of the other worlds.

Do you mean the stars?

Indeed, no.

Perhaps the world of spirits?

Nor that.

It's the city in the lights en't it?

Yes, you are correct.

How did you know that, child!?

Keep calm, she's not the only one to know of it.

Witches have known of the other worlds for thousan years. We are as close as a heartbeat, but we can touch or see or hear these other worlds . . .

. . . exce

. . . in the Northern Lights.

The Dust-hunters fear your father intends to use Dust in some way to make a bridge between this world and the world beyond the Aurora. That's why they made a pact with the armoured bears to keep him imprisoned in the fortress at Svalbard.

We have an armoure bear with us!

Do you?

Carefully with that, Szabo!

Is everything ready?

...'s the aëronaut's equipment!

...e leaving ...lvangar?

What about the bear?

I've heard tales of this bear. Iorek Byrnison is a killer and a renegade. He's outlawed from the bears' kingdom. I don't think we can trust him.

That en't true!

...sorry, Lyra, ...lvangar must ...ur priority.

The alethiometer told me. It also said where his armour is hidden.

He'll help us rescue the children . . . and my father!

Or else he'll kill us all.

WHAT THE DEVIL, SZABO! ARE YOU DOING IT ON PURPOSE?

Why does nobody ever listen?!

So have you spoken to old Iorek?

What did you say?

Lee Scoresby, aëronaut. I'm coming on the trip.

I know why you're angry, and I agree wit John Faa is wrong about the bear. I've known Iorek for years. He's a prob and no mistake, but he's loyal.

I *knew* it.

Right, but it's not going to be easy to get him away from that den of drunkards.

And you're being watched by everyone. It has to said that it's hard not to notice you and Iore

So we need to create a diversion.

SAY, ANY OF YOU GENTLEMEN IN THE MOOD FOR A GAME OF HAZARD?

I'VE GOT A FORTUNE TO LOSE!

Why don't you just make some more armour out of this metal here?

Hm?

Because this metal . . .

. . . is worthless!

My armour is sky-iron, specially made for me.

ar's armour is his soul, just your dæmon is your soul.

now where your soul is hidden.

If you're lying, you'll regret it . . .

It's the truth! I've got an alethiometer, an instrument that—

I know what an alethiometer is. If you possess one, then you must be a very special child.

Listen, they done wrong taking your armour, but you got to promise not to take vengeance.

13

No vengeance afterwards. But if they fight as I take it, they die!

It's hidden in the cellar of the priest's house. He thinks an evil spirit is inside it.

What's your name, child?

Lyra Belacqua.

I owe you a debt Lyra Belacqua

WATCH OUT!

ROAAAAARRR

NO!

Leave him alone!

CRACK

IOREK BYRNISON!

!?

15

YOU OWE ME A DEBT!

Don't fight these men. We need you, Iorek! Come away!

Come down to the harbour with me and don't even think of looking back. Farder Coram and John Faa, let them do the talking — they'll make it all right.

?!

What's all that shouting?

A riot?

Lee, what's going on?

She's unbelieva that child.

16

I don't know what's worse, the cold . . .

. . . or these never-ending fir trees.

HEY, LOOK! OVER THERE!

What?

Nothing. All these dark tree trunks are giving me the creeps.

Are you with these people?

Sure. I guess we're both hired hands.

Hired? I gave my word to the girl — there's a difference.

Ha! More like she's got one over on you.

Lyra, I want to know more about how they're defending Bolvangar. Can you see on the alethiometer?

Yes, I can see all right, Lord Faa.

They got wires all round the place . . . a company of Tartars with rifles and fire-throwers . . .

And a sort of cannon.

The Tartars, sixty of them . . . their dæmons are all wolves.

The Sibirsk regiments have wolf-dæmons! We'll have to fight like tigers.

We have an advantage: they don't real[ly] expect to be attacked.

We can't jus[t] count on surprising th[em]

The gyptians are not trained warriors. I need to think . . .

MR SCORESBY!

Wait. The alethiometer is telling me something else. In the next valley there's a village by a lake where the folk are troubled by a ghost.

I'd appreciate your advice.

It might be important.

There's bound to be s[omething] of all kinds among t[he] forests, and we've g[ot our] own troubles.

I hate it when they do that.

Grown-ups think they're so important.

The village en't far away. Maybe I could borrow a sledge?

There!

Come on! We know what to do!

18

The alethiometer is trying to tell me something I don't understand . . .

We'd better go and look.

Pan, be a bat and go and look for me.

No! It doesn't feel right! I can't!

LYRA! Don't stay here! Go back!

HEY, YOU! WHO ARE YOU?

My dæmon?

Have you got my dæmon?

20

Where is his dæmon?

The Gobblers . . .

. . . they've cut his dæmon away!

A child without a soul . . . That will be why your symbol-reader told of a ghost.

What's your name?

Tim Makarios.

NOBODY MOVE!

y! You with the bear! Are you evil spirits?

No, we're just here for the boy.

Won't need my armour, eh?

That's not a boy — it's not even a human being.

He's called Tim. He's had something horrible done to him. You should be ashamed.

There are others like him. We saw them in the forest. Sometimes they die quickly. Sometimes they don't die at all.

Take him away! Take him right away and don't come back!

Lyra, tell him to hang on.

Hold on tight to me. Go with the rhythm. You'll soon get the hang of it.

I dunno where my Ratter is. How will she find me?

We'll find her, Tim and we'll punish t Gobblers.

GRACIOUS GOD!

Is this what they are doing at Bolvangar? Cuttin away children's dæmons?

Lord Faa, forgive me for going off like that, but the alethiometer . . .

Peace, Lyra . . . it is good we know the truth.

Chief Raymond, take care of this child.

We shouldn't go near him, he will bring us bad luck.

Fine then, I'll take care o

Iorek, tell them about the army of witches please. I'm too tired to talk any more.

Come with me, Tim.

Do you think Ratter will know I'm here?

Lyra . . .

I'm afraid to tell you this after what you done, but that little boy died an hour ago.

Lyra!

No one can survive without their dæmon.

Where's his fish!?

What does it matter?

Perhaps he ate it?

DON'T YOU DARE LAUGH. I'LL TEAR YOUR LUNGS OUT IF YOU LAUGH AT HIM.

...as all he had to cling on to. Who's took it from him?

Easy, child.

I didn't know. I thought it was just what he'd been eating. I took it out of his hand because I thought it was more respectful. I gave it to my dogs.

Lend me your knife.

I hope that'll do, Tim, if I provide for you like a Jordan Scholar.

What!?

It's not stealing. This horrible spy-fly was sent for me.

u stealing Farder s sledge?

I don't want it endangering anyone else.

Do you think it can hear us?

I'll ask Iorek to weld this tight, so it doesn't open.

Have you finished it?

Yes, it's welded shut.

You'd need jaws of steel to get this open.

Thanks, Iorek. Now I know it'll be safe.

e's this, to protect your alethiometer.

Thank you, Iorek. It's perfect.

Is it hard, not having a dæmon? Don't you get lonely?

Bears are made to be solitary.

Even the Svalbard bears?

I'm not a Svalbard bear now.

Lee . . .

Could you carry Iorek and his armour in your balloon?

I have done it.

I rescued him one time from the Tartars — they had him trapped and were starving him out.

Bears aren't made to
but Lee saved me that

...you know the Tartars [ma]ke holes in people's [hea]ds?

Oh, sure. They've been doing that for thousands of years.

First they cut a half-circle of skin on the scalp, then they cut a little circle of bone out of the skull, very carefully so they don't penetrate the brain . . .

. . . then they sew it up.

[I t]hought they [di]d it to their enemies!

Hell, no. It's called trepanning, and it's a great privilege. They do it so the gods can talk to them.

Then that must mean Stanislaus Grumman was a friend of the Tartars, because he had a hole in his skull.

The explorer Grumman? Do you know him?

[I] saw his head. My father found it in the ice and showed it [t]o the Scholars at Jordan College. The Tartars had cut a [ho]le in his skull! When they saw that, the Scholars gave him all the money he needed for his expedition.

That can't be right. The Tartars don't trepan their enemies, they scalp them. Your father might have been misleading the Scholars.

[It m]ight not have been Grumman's head. [La]st we heard, he was living among Tartar tribes on the [Yeni]sei River.

He set them up?

Your father's a cunning man.

Yeah. He could easily fool a bunch of Scholars.

Tomorrow we'll reach Bolvangar.

JOHN FAA!

There's a f[...]
coming i[...]

Our reconnaissance trip to Bolvangar will be difficult right now.

Wait . . .

Lyra!

Can you tell us how long this fog will last?

OH NO!

What?

TCHAK!

!?

TCHAK!

TO ARMS!

They're cutting us to pieces — we have to fight back!

TAKE COVER BEHIND THE SLEDGES!

If only I had a revolver . . .

Why not wish for a cannon while you're at it?

IOREK!

Lyra!

AAARGH!

NO! PUT ME DOWN!

IOREK!

You name?

LET ME GO!

You name? You tell!

Lyr . . . er . . . Lizzie Brooks.

And you, who are you?

We Samoyed hunters. Who these peoples with you?

Traders.

Traders? With panserbjørn?

Yes . . . for protection.

Didn't work! Ha, ha, bear no good!

Good joke. Ha ha!

Where are you taking me?

We take you nice place. Nice food, warm bed. Nice peoples.

My friends. They'll find you and they'll kill you.

Lyra . . . They killed John Faa. I saw him go down.

I've got a bad feeling about this.

Have you still got the alethiometer with you?

It's in my coat . . . and the spy-fly tin is in my boot.

Lost child. Bring to you.

Good work, Chief.

You speak English?

Yes.

Come in quickly.

We'll look after you here, don't worry.

So this is Bolvangar?

What's your name, dear?

Lizzie. Er... Lizzie Brooks.

Come with me, c

We need to pretend to be stupid and dim, Lyra . . .

You look healthy enough How old are you?

I'm ele

Off with your clothes and we'll pop you in the shower. You're a bit whiffy.

Small for your age, aren't you?

Put these on.

I'd rather wear my own.

Later maybe.

When we've given them a good wash.

What's this?

...thing.

Just a sort of toy.

That's pretty, isn't it? It's like a compass.

It's a toy.

It's mine.

Wouldn't you rather have a nice woolly bear? Or a pretty doll?

Keep calm, Ly . . . Lizzie.

Here you are, dear.

Thank you. Can I keep my own toy too?

Yes, dear. Now get dressed.

I don't like people looking at me when . . .

Hurry up then, I haven't got all day.

Yes, Nurse.

I'm ready now.

You must be hungry.

Where are the others?

Come over here.

Eat. It's good, I promise.

You're a lucky little girl, Lizzie. Those huntsmen brought you to the best place you could be.

They never found me. They kidnapped me.

Oh, I don't think so.

I think you wandered off, and the huntsmen found you on your own and brought you here.

I saw a fight, with peop getting killed.

You *thought* you did.

That often happens in the intense cold: you fall asleep and have bad dreams and you can't remember what's true and what isn't.

THEY WERE MY FRIENDS!

Have you got parents, Lizzie?

My father, he . . . he . . .

I'm sure your father will come and find you. Until then, Nurse Clara will show you to the dormitory. You must be tired.

I'm not tired . . .

They gave her sleeping pills. Must've . . .

Wake up! Wake up!

Where am I?

They always do that to new ones, to calm 'em down.

36

...hey call this the ...erimental Station.

But really they're Gobblers. We're all going to die.

Don't tell her that! Not yet.

Don't listen to them, they're talking rubbish. It's all right here. They feed us well and they're kind. Especially Mrs Coulter.

Mrs COULTER!?

Yes, she'll be back soon.

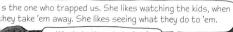

...s the one who trapped us. She likes watching the kids, when ...hey take 'em away. She likes seeing what they do to 'em.

What do they do to 'em?

They measure your Dust. If you en't got any, that's good, but everyone gets Dust in the end.

They're always on about Dust. And our dæmons.

...nd that's just at the ...ning. But afterwards they ...e you off and you're never seen again.

THAT'S NOT TRUE!

Yes it is: this boy Simon told me.

Is there boys here as well?

New kids arrive every day. Girls and boys.

Roger.

Where are you?

37

John Faa was hit by an arrow — I saw him fall.

That doesn't mean he's dead. It was very foggy, you couldn't see clearly.

Why don't you ask the alethiometer?

Too risky to get it out here! Anyway, nothing will stop Iorek. He'll rescue us. Then we'll fly to Svalbard in Lee Scoresby's balloon, to rescue my father.

You're forgetting Mrs Coulter.

I'm not forgetting her, Pan. And that's exactly why I'm calling myself Lizzie.

I hate porridge.

Lizzie, look who's behind you.

Roger!

FOOD FIGH[T]

STOP THIS AT ONCE!

!?

Lyra!

They've caught you too, Lyra?

Yes, but . . .

You got to call me Lizzie, *never* Lyra. I'll explain why later.

Er . . . OK.

. . . en, Lizzie: they cut your dæmon away . . . m you here, to see if you die or not.

Have you seen them do it?

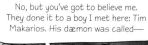

No, but you've got to believe me. They done it to a boy I met here: Tim Makarios. His dæmon was called—

She was called Ratter. Tim died. We buried him.

. . . buried . . . im?

I'll tell you later. Where is it they do their experiments?

In another building. I heard they make a hole in your head.

We've got to escape. Do you know if Billy Costa is here?

. . . es . . . and I found a hiding place. There's a space above the ceiling panels. They just lift up and you can crawl in.

YOU, COME WITH ME!

39

I can't think why you started all that, but don't expect me to feel sorry for you.

And after that, you can clean the dining room and then it's back to your room . . . and no supper for you!

I thought you said it wasn't safe to use the alethiometer here!

Shush! I'm trying to concentrate.

Lyr . . . Lizzie?

BILLY! How did you . . . ?

Through the ceiling.

Roger said you wanted to see me.

Billy Costa! You bet I wanted to see you! Your brother's coming, and John Faa and a whole band of gyptians. They're going to take you home.

I knew it. When will they get here?

I'll know soon. But you'd better go now. They mustn't find you here.

Who was that boy?

!!

What boy?

This is the girls' dormitory.

Do you think I'm stupid?

Of course not.

I think you know all about things that go on here.

They all think I'm st[?] because I'm fat, but I [?] a lot more [?] they think

Listen, there's a building that's different from the othe[?]

40

DRRRRRRRrrrrrrrrrrrrrrrrrrrrrrrrRRRRRRRRRRRRRRRRR

THE FIRE ALARM!

Quick, get your coat and boots!

I en't got any. They took my stuff away!

rrRRRRRRRRRRRRRRRRRRRRRR RRRRRRRRRRRRRRRRRRRRRRRR

!?

RRRRRRRRRRRRRRRRRRRRRRRRRRRRRRRRRRRRRRRRRRRRRRRRRRR

Take your things, you silly girl!

LISTEN TO ME, CHILDREN.

THERE'S NO FIRE! THIS IS A NEW EXERCISE.

rrRRRRRRRRRRRRRRRRRRRR RRRRRRRRRRRRRRRRRRRRRRRRRRRRRRRRRR

YOU NEED TO LEARN HOW TO DRESS WARMLY . . .

See that big building? That's where they do the experiments.

That's where I'm going, then.

. . . AND HOW TO MAKE A CALM EXIT, WHEN YOU HEAR THE ALARM . . .

You're crazy!

Help me — they mustn't spot me.

41

Darn, it's locked.

LOOK, A BIRD!

ra! I knew I'd find
u here! What are
you doing?

KAISA!

Why are you trying
to get in there?

Because of what they do here. They cut
children's dæmons away. And I think
maybe they do it in here.

Who is he?

is the witch Serafina
ekkala's dæmon.

A dæmon on its own?

nd back.
en the door.

CLICK!

I've never seen
magic before!

ve got to hurry. They'll notice we're
missing soon.

GO, KAROSSA!

ORDER!

FLATTEN HER,
KYRILLION!

I WILL HAVE ORDER!

43

Pass the word around among all the kids. They got to know where the outdoor clothes are and be ready to run as soon as we give the signal.

What's the signal?

STOP THIS NOISE IMMEDIATELY!

The fire bell. When the time comes, I'll set it off.

THAT'S ENOUGH!

I'M WARNING YOU . . .

THERE WILL BE REPERCUSSIONS!

THE FIRE DRILL IS OVER. LINE UP GET BACK TO YOUR ROOMS. IN SI

What pandemonium! I thought you should all know better than to behave like that!

?!

46

We are about to arrive, Mrs Coulter.

You think you're so clever, don't you? Well, I'm watching you, Lizzie Brooks. We'll see how long that lasts.

Not this disgusting porridge again!

Can't they come up with anything else?

Thanks for your help the other day.

Things have certainly livened up since you arrived.

Tell us what you saw in that building. Was I right about it?

It's even worse.

But it'll soon be over . . . People are coming to rescue us. They'll be here tomorrow. Or maybe even sooner.

OH!

She's come back. She's so beautiful.

Do you get enough to eat here?

Yes, Miss. Did you send my letter to my mother and father?

Of course. I'm sure they'll write back soon.

She's coming over! Do something!

!?

Lizzie! Are you mad?

Ha ha ha!

Well?!

I, er . . .

Excuse me . . .

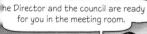

The Director and the council are ready for you in the meeting room.

That monkey, he's the *worst* . . . He attacked my Karossa and nearly killed him. I wasn't strong enough. That's how she caught me.

That's how she caught us all.

What's this meeting room?

They took me there one time . . .

There were about twenty of them in there. She was there too.

One of them was giving a lecture, and I had to do everything they asked.

They took my dæmon away, even though that's not allowed. And they pulled us as far apart as they could.

49

I've never been in so much pain.

Where are you going, Lizzie?

I'll be back.

Lyra, no!

Remember what happened last time you played your spying games?

All we have to do is wait patiently for John Faa and Iorek to come and rescue us.

Shush! I'm trying to get my bearings.

The alarm systems didn't work.

Was it sabotage? How do you explain this? Don't you have someone guarding the laboratory?

Who else could it be?

It might have been done a child. One of them co have made the most o the mayhem.

Come, come, you surely don't suspect one of the staff?

What a mess! But enough of that for now. Tell me about the new separator.

Actually, a curious discovery by Lord Asriel gave us the key to a new meth He discovered that an alloy of manganese and titanium has the property insulating body from dæmon.

detachment is clean and simple ...ess trauma ... only five-per-cent ...ath rate ... anbaric scalpel ...

No! They won't do it to us — we won't let them ...

We've developed a new separator. A kind of guillotine, I suppose you could say ...

The child is placed in a compartment of alloy mesh, with the dæmon in a similar connecting compartment. Then a blade is brought down between them, severing the link.

I should like to see this as soon as possible.

But I'm tired now. I think I'll go to bed.

Tell us, Mrs Coulter ...

... what has happened to Lord Asriel?

Despite being in exile in Svalbard, Lord Asriel continues to ...ursue his heretical experiments. The Consistorial Court of Discipline expects him to be executed.

Does that satisfy your curiosity, Dr Cooper?

It does, Mrs Coulter.

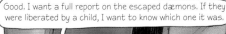

Good. I want a full report on the escaped dæmons. If they were liberated by a child, I want to know which one it was.

Of course, I disapprove of Lord Asriel's theories . . .

. . . but her attitude worries me . . . A *personal* interest which is almost ghoulish.

Hush! Not so loud.

Father Jones is right.

Do you remember those first experiments, when she was so keen to see them pulled apart . . . ?

LIZZIE!?

Dirty little . . . Ouch!

STOP HER!

OWWW!

Who is this child?

The new one.

You don't suppose *she* . . . the dæmons . . . ?

Could well be. But not on her own, surely?

e can't go back with the other ren. Only one thing we *can* do . . .

Can't leave it till the morning. Mrs Coulter wants to watch.

Do it now and perhaps the Oblation Board need not know about the slip-up.

Quick, she's waking up!

PANTALAIMON!

Noo . . .

NO! LET ME GO!

55

My dear, dear child, however did you come to be here?

Did you get lost? Did someone take you out of the flat?

We're only sa[fe] as long as we pretend.

Watch the monkey. He'll want the alethiometer.

A man and a woman took me. Guests at the party, I think. They lured me downstairs and put me in a car.

I managed to escape, but I didn't kn[ow] where I was. I was trying to find my [way] back, only these Gobblers caught [me] and put me on a ship and I do[n't] know where we went then[.]

My poor darling. Were they the ones who brought you here?

No, first they drove me to the North . . .

GRRRRRRR

. . . and I escaped from them there, but then Samoyed hunters captured m[e] and sold me to the people here.

It was horrible! They were going to — going to cut— But why? I never done anything wrong!

There, there . . . You're safe, my dear. No one's going to harm you, Lyra darling.

GRRRRRR

But they do it to other children! Why? It's because of Dust, isn[']t[?]

Ah, my love . . .

Well, actually . . .

They only do it for the children's own good.

56

Dust is something evil and dangerous. Grown-ups and their dæmons are infected with Dust so deeply that it's too late for them. But a quick operation on children means Dust won't stick to them ever again. They're safe and—

No one would take a child's dæmon away altogether! All that happens is a little cut, and then everything's peaceful. Just one little cut, and they don't really feel it. Their dæmons are still with them, but not connected. It's as if . . .

Speak for yourself, you nauseating brute!

As if you had a wonderful pet. The best pet in the world! Wouldn't you like that?

And there's one other thing, Lyra dear. I think the Master of Jordan College gave you something before you left. He told you not to tell me about it, didn't he?

can see you're worried that I've ssed your secret. Well, never mind, rling, because you *didn't* tell me, did you?

Get lost!

But it wasn't his to give . . . So it really would be better to let me have it, don't you think?

RHHHHHHH

The alethiometer is a very old and precious object.

So rare, in fact, that very few people have ever seen one. And they're not for children, really, either. Will you let me look after it? — And what is that funny thing?

What a funny old tin! What have you got in there, dear? It's welded. Open it, Ozymandias!

AAAAGH!

WHAT IS IT?

LYRA, WAIT . . .

MY GOD, THE SPY-FLY!

LYRA!

DRRRRRRRRRRRRRRRRRRRRRRRRRRRRRRRRRRRRR

RRRRRRRR RRRRRRRR RRRRRRRR RRRRRRRR RRRRRRRRR

RRRRRRRR RRRRRRRR RRRRRRRR RRRRRRRR RRRRRRRRRRRRRR

UTSIDE, EVERYONE!

TAKE YOUR COATS!

RRRRRRRRR RRRRRRRR RRRRRRRR RRRRRRRR RRRRRRRRR RRRRRRRR

EP CALM!
MEMBER
HE FIRE
DRILL!

LIZZIE!

RRRRRRRRRRRRRRRRRRRRRRRRRRRRRRRRRRRRRRR

e are the gyptians
are supposed to be
rescuing us?

I don't
know.

I had no choice.

What? Then why
the alarm?

WHAM!

LISTEN, EVERYONE!

WE'VE GOT TO RUN FOR OUR LIVES!

FOLLOW THE LIGHTS – THEY LEAD TO THE GATE!

STOP!

We're done for.

No we're not! Watch me.

TAKE THAT!

Billy, you're going to get us all killed.

Do you think this is a game?

AT MY COMMAND . . .

THWACK!

THE WITCHES ARE HELPING US — RUN!

Devil!

Lyra, look out!

IOREK!

Follow my tracks, I'll lead you to the gyptians!

CRASH!

COME ON!

Where are we going?

I don't know, just follow...

I can't feel my feet any more.

I want to go back to the station. It was warm there.

Come on, Martha!

Get moving, idiot!

Do you think the Gobblers will welcome you back with tea and biscuits?

HEY, LOOK: A SECOND SUN!

No, it's . . .

LEE SCORESBY!

THANKS FOR THE GAS!

CRACK!

PUT IT ON MY ACCOUNT!

BLAM

It's snowing — Iorek's tracks will get covered up.

What could be worse than that?

WOLVES!

KEEP TOGETHER, OR YOU'LL GET LOST!

TCHAK

LYRA, GATHER UP THE CHILDREN AND HEAD FOR THE LIGHTS!

65

So this is the famous Roger. The one you came here to get.

Yes . . .

. . . and we're going back to Jordan College together, once we've rescued my father.

Your father?

Who is your father?

Lord Asriel. And Mrs Coulter is my mot[her]

What? Why didn't you tel[l] me before?

I haven't known very long.

But if you'd rather go back to Jordan College on your own . . .

After all you've done for me? Do you take me for a coward?

We knew you were alive. The goose Kaisa came to tell us.

Yes, and we rescued all the dæmons in the laboratory.

Lyra did that. You [are] just shaking with [terror?]

Did you use the mechanical beetle wisely?

How did you know that I'd used it didn't mean to, but I'll tell you what happened . . .

. . . the beetle leapt into the face of Mrs Coulter's dæmon. I don't know if my mother is dead or injured.

Farder Coram, I took the beetle to protect you. All of you.

Well, let's hope it was destroyed in the explosion.

!?

CRASH

OWWWW!

And now, you little pest . . .

. . . you are coming with me!

NO!
LET ME GO!

TARTAR WARRIORS! KILL
THE GYPTIANS!

BANG!

BANG!

BANG!

!?

ROAAAAAR

Hey!

Who are you?

Medea. I'm a witch.

Pantalaimon!

Perhaps the first one you've met?

I was shouting 'filthy witch' earlier . . . I'm so sorry.

She's a friend, Roger!

And now, jump!

What! You can't mean it! I said I was sorry!

Trust me – go on, ju

They're going to break their necks!

Skip inside, quick!

Cast off, folks!

BANG

How dare they use a damned panserbjørn! Yo arrived just in time. Now, FINISH HIM OF

70

Lee, they've got a machine gun!

GOOD GRIEF!

IOREK, GET OUT OF THERE!

!?

WHAT ARE YOU DOING, YOU IMBECILE!?

I can't help it. It's jammed! It's the cold . . .

Click!

Click!

Hold on tight, folks . . .

C'mon, Iorek!

Yep! Now we're full up!

BANG!

BANG!

Greetings, my old friend.

!?

BANG!

SERAFINA!

BANG!

BANG!

I can't bear you to look at me — I'm an old man now.

But your heart is so strong I can hear it beating.

ROOOOOOOOOOOO...

Farewell... Watch over Lyra.

THE TARTARS ARE ON THE RUN!

HURRAH!

Wrap yourselves up in these furs before you turn into icicles.

Mr Scoresby, how did you find us?

Witches. And there's one witch-lady who wants to talk to you.

Here she comes now — Serafina!

Lyra?

Mr Scoresby says you want to go to Svalbard, to Lord Asriel. Why?

To take him the alethiometer, of course!

Or... to help him escape... try anyway.

Yes, that's it!

73

If that is the case, there are things I need to tell you.

About Dust?

Yes, among other things. But you are tired now, and it will be a long flight. We'll talk when you wake up.

I'm not . . . tired . . .

To be continued . . .

ALSO BY PHILIP PULLMAN

His Dark Materials
Northern Lights
The Subtle Knife
The Amber Spyglass

Northern Lights – The Graphic Novel: Volume One

Lyra's Oxford
Once Upon a Time in the North
The Collectors

The Sally Lockhart Quartet
The Ruby in the Smoke
The Shadow in the North
The Tiger in the Well
The Tin Princess

The Adventures of the New Cut Gang
Thunderbolt's Waxwork
The Gas-Fitters' Ball

Fairy Tales
The Firework-Maker's Daughter
Clockwork
I Was a Rat!
The Scarecrow and His Servant

Other Books
Count Karlstein
Count Karlstein (graphic novel)
Spring-Heeled Jack
Aladdin
Mossycoat
Puss in Boots
Grimm Tales: For Young and Old
The Broken Bridge
The Butterfly Tattoo
The Good Man Jesus and the Scoundrel Christ

Plays
Frankenstein (adaptation)
Sherlock Holmes and the Limehouse Horror